"LIFE GOES ON..."

Roger Guest

authorHOUSE®

"LIFE GOES ON..."

A sequel to LET`S MAKE LIKE LUCAN...
Another adventure with Gil Lamont and Amentrude
Chemin...

A story of covert investigation to uncover an
international network involving Illegal arms dealing,
the fight against the proliferation of high tech
weaponry , and the use of chemical and biological
weapons by terrorist groups .

BADGER

AuthorHouse™ UK
1663 Liberty Drive
Bloomington, IN 47403 USA
www.authorhouse.co.uk
Phone: 0800.197.4150

Published by AuthorHouse   02/16/2015

ISBN: 978-1-5049-3760-3 (sc)
ISBN: 978-1-5049-3761-0 (e)

FOREWORD

Gil Lamont is a retired Detective Sergeant in the US Army CIS.

After the pursuit of a fraudulent financial advisor to recover his life savings, he finds a hopefully more peaceful life in Paris with a beautiful Interpol Agent named Armentrude Chemin, but gets inexorably involved in another exploit.

The story is fiction, and bears no relation to any persons living or dead.

The author is a retired aerospace engineer. His interests include sailing, scuba diving, fishing and the natural environment.

LIFE GOES ON . . . How Gil Lamont and his new friend Armentrude Chemin try to settle down after the turbulence of their first meeting.

CONTENTS

LIST OF CHARACTERS

Gil Lamont	Investigator & MCIS veteran.
Armentrude Chemin	Interpol Agent.
Giles Greenaway	British entrepreneur and UK Advisor on Security.
Senior Sergeant Valery Stensis	French Foreign Legion and Double Agent.
Gerard	Corsican owner of "Chez Doumé" Restaurant.
US Army General Sherman Blund	US Homeland Security Duty Officer of the Watch.
Commandant Victor Pintonen	French Foreign Legion Commander Calvi Fortress.
Abdul Salim	Terrorist Group Commander, Al Qaeda.
Grey haired man with spectacles	MI6 Agent.
Admiral Walter Revere USN	Chairman of the US Homeland Defence Committee.
The President of The United States of America.	
Boss	SAS Communications Officer.
Mike	SAS Lieutenant.
Jim	SAS Weapons Specialist.
Bill	SAS Explosives Specialist.
Nick	Belgian Special Forces.
Lieutenant Yuri Thorniloe	Israeli Air Force helicopter pilot.
Professor Henri Zinn	Sagol School of Neuroscience, Tel-Aviv University.
Dr. Ilia Zagreb	Tel-Aviv University Center for Nanoscience.
Dexter Main	Fishing Boat Skipper, Nassau.

LIFE GOES ON . . . Gil and Armentrude reflect on the Luccombe saga.

Chapter 1
THE HOLIDAY

At their Paris apartment, investigator Gil Lamont and his lover Interpol Agent Armentrude Chemin lay in bed reflecting on the news that fugitive Rory Luccombe had been killed by his jilted girlfriend Francoise Bateille, whilst handcuffed to two Scotland Yard Detectives during a trans-Atlantic flight.

"That bastard turned my life inside out. I lost my money, my job, and worst of all my life-long partner Mary-Jane. I guess that I, we, collected considerable funds during his pursuit, and I got to meet you . . . but for all that effort, risk and violence, the due process of Law was not achieved. I suppose that I am fortunate not to be charged with murder myself . . . but McNeish killed Jim Silt", he added swiftly, being careful not to refer to the two dead Mafiosi in the Paris car park . . . "The good thing is that *we* met!".

Armentrude remained silent, but realised that she felt safe and happy beside him. She had only recently started at Interpol, having graduated from the Sorbonne. Her association with Gil Lamont had launched her into the deep end of international crime so soon in her career. She had found the experience exciting, but she felt drained.

She was due some leave, so she suggested that they should take a holiday together.

"I will book an Air Inter flight to Nice, because we get a cheaper ticket if I book through Interpol. We can then take the fast ferry to Calvi where my parents have a holiday apartment. Calvi is beautiful, and I adore arriving at an island by sea . . . it is *so* romantic!"

"Will your parents be there?" . . . a natural male caution set in, but Gil was not too worried, parents were hardly serious protagonists.

"No, they are in Canada with my uncle in Quebec . . . When a ship arrives at a harbour, particularly an island harbour, I love to see the anticipation and excitement in the faces of the crowd which always attends the arrival of a ferry. It is so welcoming, particularly in the evening".

Gil had no answer to that, but put it down to his overall fascination for this seemingly exotic young woman. He could see no reason why they could not fly direct to Calvi, but did not object to the sea trip if that was what she wanted.

At his tropical hideaway in Deadman`s Cay, Giles Greenaway heaved a sigh of relief on learning of the death of his associate Rory Luccombe . . .

`What a stroke of luck!`, he thought.

Now the risk of embarrassing questions was much reduced. However, there remained the problem of this annoying American, Gil Lamont and his Interpol girlfriend. They had accepted his inducement not to pursue Rory Luccombe, but had continued to do so! However, they had the support of Interpol, the FBI, and begrudgingly HMRC and the Home Secretary. It was unlikely that he could recoup his quarter of a million dollars from the Special Investigations Account of Interpol Paris. He would have to think of some way of explaining this expenditure. Not really a problem . . . merely a question of manipulating budgets ; easily done at his level. *After all, it was only Tax Payers` money* . . . he thought without the slightest twinge of conscience.

But I wonder how much he knows about my involvement, or will he just let things go and enjoy life with his beautiful girlfriend? I think I should keep tabs on him for the next six months.

He sent a request for an Operative to MI6. Someone who could track Lamont remotely, and who was capable of handling himself if confrontation was necessary.

Meanwhile, Gil and Armentrude had flown to Nice, and taken a taxi to the Ferry Terminal in the old port of Nice. They took the high speed ferry to Calvi, some one hundred and sixty kilometres south of Nice in Corsica. It was dusk as they disembarked, and Gil sensed the excitement in Armentrude as they climbed up the street from the ferry terminal to the main town beyond the enormous fortress which was the Head Quarters of the French Foreign Legion. This military organisation was formed from a dissolute group of men from many different nations who were trained as special forces, and bludgeoned into a fighting force by the extreme discipline of the French Army. Experts in desert and jungle warfare, they were intensely involved with African forces in support of United Nations operations right across the Southern Sahara against the "Ganjaweed" armed terror groups trained and sponsored in part by Al Qaeda. These predominantly Muslim groups burned, raped and slaughtered any settled communities from Sudan to Senegal.

As they walked down into the main part of Calvi situated on an elegantly curved bay with a Marina and golden sandy beach beyond, they passed busy bars and restaurants in which were off-duty Legionnaires, impeccably smart in their uniforms. Gil remarked on this, because American servicemen usually changed into civilian clothes when off-duty.

Armentrude replied that Legionnaires were discouraged from having personal effects, and had to wear uniform at all times. This promoted an impression of instant readiness.

"I think you have a secret admiration, a schoolgirl infatuation with these guys", said Gil in a provocatively joking way . . .

Armentrude blushed . . . "Why not?", she said. "I think they are marvellous!. They hunt down the terror gangs and destroy them".

"I heard that the "Ganjaweed" are mostly kids between nine and fourteen years old", jibed Gil, winding her up . . .

"If you give a child a Kalashnikov and tell him to kill or have his hands cut off, he becomes an extremely dangerous opponent. In any case, they are lead by well trained, self appointed `Colonels` who are murderous psychopaths".

"I hope that`s not why we came here", observed Gil, "I thought this was meant to be a peaceful holiday!"

"Of course, but I love everything about Corsica, and the Legion dominates Calvi, which I think is the most beautiful town in the world, and because of them, one of the safest".

They found the family apartment situated on the Rue Georges Clemenceau, facing south across the bay, with a view of the mountains which formed the spine of the island beyond. After a quick shower and a change into a diaphanous little number, Armentrude said "now let me show you Corsican delight number one" . . .

This briefly grabbed Gil's attention, but she went on to describe the Corsican cuisine, saying that her favourite restaurant was quite close, and that she was ravenous . . .

"Eat first, and the rest comes after".

"I don't need a rest" said Gil, "and I'm not too hungry", but dodging his attempted embrace, she ran down the stairs and out into the road.

She led him to an un-assuming restaurant called "Chez Doumé, Specialistes Corse" in the same street.

Sitting in the corner was a lone Legionnaire, eating his meal in silence. Gil had to admit that he was immaculate. His shoes were so highly polished that they immediately focussed one's attention. His closely cropped hair was perhaps two millimetres long at best, showing his sun-tanned scull beneath. On both scarred fore-arms he had a small tattoo, discretely indicating some obscure allegiance. His eyes were steely grey in an emotionless face looking diagonally across the room so that he could see everything without turning his head whilst eating. His desert brown uniform was impeccably pressed. Gil was not sure of his rank, but he appeared to be some sort of senior under-officer. He was probably about forty years old, two metres tall and about a hundred and ninety pounds of muscle. He was eating a very rare steak and drinking mineral water. As a Senior Master Sergeant himself, Gil could not remember any of his company who did not take at least a beer with their food.

The owner of the restaurant greeted them, embracing Armentrude and ushering them to a table.

"Ah mademoiselle, you have now become so beautiful since I last saw you", said Gerard, the owner of the restaurant.

Embarrassed, Gil said "good evening" to the two men, but the Legionnaire ignored him, showing no indication that he had seen or heard them.

"Un petit boisson de maison", said Gerard, producing two of his special version of a kia, an aperitif of white wine and black-current cordial with herbs and ice. A wonderful smell of cooking filled the room and Armentrude immediately ordered a tagine of wild boar, two carafes of house red and a bottle of eau gazeuse, which arrived with an enormous basket of fresh bread. The room was painted white with primitive art on the walls, adding a note of colour and warmth.

"Isn't he wonderful" she whispered, nodding towards the Legionnaire, "they are all like that!".

Gil said, "I doubt it, but I am getting slightly concerned about your obvious obsession".

"Now you are jealous", she laughed. Gil smiled, but said nothing.

"Don't be jealous darling, since I met you, you have accomplished some astonishing things and you are obviously proud of your American military background, but I wanted to show you that in France, we too have some very special forces, some say the best in the world".

"They all say that, the Israelis, the SAS, the Navy Seals, the royal Marines and the Russians, but I am retired . . . a tired old veteran, a retard I guess. I just want to live quietly. *You* are the spook, not me", said Gil who for some reason felt inadequately dressed in his jeans and holiday shirt in the presence of this formidable soldier. He realised for the first time since leaving the MCIS, how proud he had been of his United States Army Uniform, and that Armentrude had never seen him wearing it.

`Get real!`, he said to himself, `it`s the man *in* the uniform that counts. I must be very tired to be having such adolescent thoughts`, but he had to admit that he was impressed by the invincible aura of the Legionnaire.

Soon the bread and wine, and the fact that he was in the company of the most devastatingly beautiful woman that he had ever met, restored his confidence.

"Damn, I`m a lucky son of a bitch", he said out loud, "I never had wild boar before, but this tagine is delicious".

Gerard joined them at the table, bringing a copious cheese board and a bunch of grapes, accompanied with a bottle of Marquis de Montesquiou Grande Reserve Armagnac.

"You will need coffee with this", he said as the restaurant began to fill up, "now my wife will take charge of affaires, and you must tell me of your adventures in your new job". He filled a glass with Armagnac and consumed it in one draft.

A duet of folksingers arrived and the Legionnaire departed without saying a word. The evening became more convivial, and they all sang the choruses, even though Gil did not understand a word of the songs. Gil could not remember paying the bill as they staggered home to their apartment.

"I could get to enjoy this!", he said as he fell asleep in Armentrude`s arms.

Deep beneath a mountain somewhere in Wyoming, the Chiefs of Staff of the United States of America were watching a real-time transmission from a military satellite passing over North Africa. They were wondering if they should alert the President because some unusual activity was developing. A group of several suspected terrorists had been tracked from Europe and the Far East to a desert training area, believed to be controlled by Al Qaeda.

After several weeks, they had suddenly all embarked in trucks with some twenty other armed men and were heading north across the Sahara to an unknown destination. The problem was that the satellite was moving roughly north to south and the convoy of trucks south to north, and transmission would soon be lost before its destination was known. The area to which it was heading had once been under French colonial control, but was now southern Libya, and not controlled by any effective force. However, it was deemed prudent to alert the French Authorities in Paris, who notified the French Foreign Legion Headquarters in Corsica. There had recently been an attack on a BP Oil pumping depot in the Southern Sahara area and several European workers killed. US Army General Sherman Blund was the Duty Officer of the day, and he wound-up his watch saying . . .

"Gentlemen, the situation is currently at "Developing Condition 4". If it get`s to Dev Con 2, we are required to advise the Secretary of State, who will decide whether to notify the President who will make any further decisions required. Do not hesitate to keep me up-dated of any developments, have a very good night". . . and he departed.

Chapter 2
THE GATHERING MENACE

In his fortress in Calvi, Commandant Victor Pintonen of the Foreign Legion considered this intelligence and put his rapid reaction force on "Attention Premier Niveau", pending further information as to where an attack might materialise. This could be anywhere in the Mediterranean, Europe, or the Middle East.

Commandant Pintonen hailed from Estonia, and had come south to warmer climes after the decline of the USSR in 1998. He had no living ties with his country, and he embodied all the toughness, discipline, and military expertise for which the Foreign Legion are famous.

Senior Sergeant Valery Stensis, known by his associates as "Stazi" had finished his dinner at the Restaurant Chez Doumé, and was just reviewing the tasks for the breaking day . . .

He noted the alert, picked up his telephone and said one word . . . "Dingo!"

Immediately, a bell rang in the fortress wash rooms, and two dozen Legionnaires who were in the process of shaving and showering, stopped everything and got dressed as quickly as possible. Within five minutes, they were all armed and assembled in the Fortress Briefing Room where Senior Sergeant Stensis instructed them to prepare three Puma troop carrying Helicopters, and to equip them for a mission to North Africa, and to stand-by . . .

Ninety three minutes after the satellite transmission of southern Sahara was lost, the satellite had completed its orbit and was heading south again, crossing the Algerian coast slightly to the east of its last pass. The Duty Officer in Wyoming switched on the recorder while the team scrutinised the transmission in real time, looking for the tracks of the convoy from where it had last been seen . . . No sign of the trucks!

On the ground in the desert, the terrorist leader Abdul Salim had hidden his trucks beneath sand-covered tarpaulins, and feathered the tracks in the sand to gradually disappear. He knew that eventually, expert analysers would examine the satellite pictures and locate his position, but not before the current transmission was lost, and he would be long gone . . . giving him about two hours to move towards his destination un-detected. This cat and mouse game of evasion and detection continued for two days . . .

In the mean time, Gil and Armentrude continued their idyllic holiday. They sun-bathed and swam in Calvi Bay, and took the small gauge railway service built by De Lesseps in the nineteenth century, which runs through delightful scenery the whole length of the island, and saw ancient castles and quaint towns. They listened to an organ recital in a church in Vivario, which they both felt deeply moving. Gil was surprised at himself . . . this was perhaps the first time that he had experienced that sort of emotion . . . he felt as if he might just drift away, emotionally up-lifted. They then indulged in a superb Salad Nicoise in a nearby restaurant, washed down with a carafe of very cold local rosée.

"Its almost like we just got married!" said Armentrude . . . Gil was shaken into reality. He could not believe that this fantastic girl could consider him as a suitable lifetime partner.

Then `perhaps`, he thought, `the young generation did not think that far ahead`.

`Well let`s enjoy it while it lasts`, he concluded.

On the evening of fourth day, the Restaurant "Chez Doumé" was full of Legionnaires. The ambiance had changed . . . the men sitting together, eating and talking quietly with Senior Sergeant Valery Stensis. No music played. In the far right hand corner sat an unassuming man with horn-rimmed spectacles and rather long grey hair. Gil had not seen him before.

"Its like the Last Supper", Gil remarked, "what are they saying? . . . some of them have camouflage grease on . . . the ones with light skin!"

Armentrude whispered, "They think that their target may be fast boats leaving the port of Skikda in Algeria . . . they hope to attack them before they embark" . . .

Immediately, Sergeant Stensis stood up, saying "Attention, silence!" to his men, and advancing towards Gil, said in English, "I apologise for my men. You, I suspect will have noticed that they are excited, perhaps even nervous. You have of course heard nothing. We know that you are an American soldier. Repeating anything you have heard tonight could be fatal! *You*, of course, will understand. Good night Monsieur", and with that they all left.

Armentrude was shocked and indignant . . . "That was intolerable", she exploded . . .

"Calm down", said Gil . . . and Gerard came bustling across to their table . . .

"Please Mademoiselle Armentrude, this little restaurant is like a home to these poor soldiers and just sometimes their stressful lifestyle causes them to say unfortunate things, but they are heroes, looking after our security . . . you must be aware that for centuries, this little island has been attacked by corsairs from North Africa, and these brave men come here to defend us and the honour of France!"

"Jesus", muttered Gil, shaking his head, and they resumed their meal. The quiet man in the corner remained impassive.

Chapter 3
THE STORM BREAKS

Off a quiet beach near Skikida, six fast boats waited for a signal from the dark shoreline.

Ashore, Abdul Salim and his men had arrived as yet undetected. Embittered rather than educated, now he could reveal to them their mission . . . "Tonight and for as long as it takes, we will attack the centre of the infidels' tourism in Southern Europe. Colonial France, our oppressors have for years inhabited Corsica, reserving it as their own private retreat for dissipation, May Allah be with you".

Each boat was armed with twin 30mm heavy calibre machine guns, and in a calm sea could sustain 55 knots with six men on board.

At 03.00 hours three Puma helicopters started their engines, and Gil heard them as he lay beside the sleeping Armentrude in Calvi. He recalled those nights in 'nam and Afghanistan, visions of bits of bodies . . . of screaming children . . . of burning flesh . . .

As the sound of the helicopters receded, he wondered how they would deal with whatever was developing. He was so glad that he was no longer involved in the Military.

At 04.00 hours, flying at 150 knots at a height of 65 metres, the three Pumas had skirted Sardinia, and were approaching Algerian Air Space. The Puma crews strained their eyes though the breaking dawn, looking for a group of fast boats, or any suspicious vessels which might hold the terrorist group. The course and destination of their target boats was unknown, so it was important to catch them as early as possible, before they had finished embarking the terrorist force.

As the sun's rays broke the horizon, they lit-up the wakes of six fast boats heading north. A large modern motor yacht lay ahead of them, distant five clicks. Senior Sergeant Stensis ordered Puma number three to descend, identify and interrogate the motor yacht, and to warn it of a possible pirate attack, whilst he and the second Puma went on to intercept the six fast boats.

Puma Three hovered near the motor yacht, hailing them on Channel 16, and by loud hailer. No response . . . and no sign of crew. They reported and waited for instructions from Puma One, but Pumas One and Two were engaging the flotilla of fast boats.

Now Abdul Salim immediately ordered his boats to fan-out as far as possible, to give each the widest possible arc of fire without hitting one another.

The Pumas were not attack helicopters, and could not engage these targets effectively with all their fire power. They were extremely vulnerable to the 30 mm machine guns on the fast boats. However, Puma Two sank one boat with an RPG fired through its open side door before being hit by machine gun fire from the remaining boats. Puma One was also hit, suffering loss of power in one engine whilst giving covering fire to Puma Two.

On the motor yacht, a single crew member appeared on the rear deck. Puma Three came in closer to communicate, but too late, saw that he was carrying a shoulder-launched Stinger missile. At close range, the missile destroyed the Puma and all its occupants.

Pumas One and Two headed for the nearest land which was Sardinia, where they made emergency landings on this Italian Island. From Puma One, Sergeant Stensis sent a sit rep to Commandant Pintonen in Calvi, requesting recovery assistance. In Puma Two, three Legionnaires were wounded, but all would survive.

At sea, Abdul Salim recovered survivors and the five remaining fast boats headed for the motor yacht to re-group. After re-fuelling, the five fast fast boats made for sleepy Sardinia, whilst the motor yacht made quietly towards Ajaccio in Corsica, where it docked in a marina birth, ostensibly awaiting the arrival of Affairs Maritime Officers to record its presence in French waters. It was however a very hot day and siesta time, so an unknown number of terrorists had arrived in the main centre of the Corsican tourist trade un-detected. Three of them slipped ashore un-noticed, and took the train to Calvi.

The Italian authorities in Sardinia were rather stretched that afternoon as reports came in of two military helicopters making forced landings in one area, and the suspicious arrival of five armed motor boats in another. They decided to attend the helicopters first . . . after siesta . . . Long before they could find the motor boats, darkness fell and the boats departed for Corsica. Splitting up, two of them headed for Ajaccio, and three for Calvi.

As he lay on the beach in Calvi, relaxing after another good lunch, Gil suddenly experienced a feeling of apprehension. At first, he could not identify the cause, but then he realised that he had not heard the Pumas return. He knew that even if they had stopped to refuel, they should have been back by now. A gut feeling told him that something was wrong. He told himself that a hundred things might have diverted the helicopters to another destination, but his anxiety remained. For the rest of the day and all that night, he was alert and subconsciously looking out for the unusual.

In Wyoming, the Duty Officer and his team had observed developments in the Mediterranean whenever the satellite had passed over, and notified the Fifth Fleet and Washington. At Interpol, her Section Chief recalled Armentrude to Paris, and she made arrangements for herself and Gil to fly out from Ajaccio next morning.

As they packed that night in Calvi for departure next day, there was a terrific explosion quite close in the town. Looking out across the bay, Gil could see three high speed boats racing for the beach with machine guns spraying the marina and town behind it, lines of tracer ricocheting from buildings. In the marina, yachts were burning, and some were already sunk. People screamed in the streets and houses burned. There was a smoking gap where a restaurant had been.

At last, the fortress began to return fire, directing it at the motor boats, one of which was hove-to off the beach, while the other two circled, giving covering fire. Gil realised that the stationary boat was waiting to embark the terrorists who had planted the bomb.

"Oh man! . . . I need a gun, have you got a gun in the house?" he shouted, and was amazed when Armentrude appeared with a sporting rifle and a box of rounds.

"My father hunts wild boar!" she said, as if an explanation was required . . .

Gil sighted on the bow of the stationary boat and fired several rounds at the gun crew.

Then he saw three figures racing towards the waiting boat, pursued by Legionnaires who were clearly un-armed. He fired at the lead figure from some 700 metres, and saw the sand fly up as his round passed through the running man's legs. He aimed slightly higher at the next figure and saw him fall at the water's edge. The third man tried to assist him, but Gil cut him down with a last round before pausing to re-load. The Legionnaires rushed into the shallow water as the boat crew desperately tried to get clear and under-way, but they were quickly overwhelmed. The remaining two boats had sheered away from the fortress' guns, and they now disappeared into the night.

Meanwhile in Ajaccio, the other two motor boats had raced into the harbour, and were firing into the Sailing Club building by the marina, and at anyone moving on the harbour side, causing such distress and confusion that nobody noticed that the motor yacht had fired three anti-tank weapons into the side of an enormous cruise liner at its water-line, and several rocket propelled grenades into its superstructure, causing fires and many casualties.

Within minutes, it was obvious that the massive ship was taking water fast and listing. Shortly after, it settled on the seabed of the harbour.

Alerted by Interpol and alarming reports from Corsica, the French Authorities had despatched the aircraft carrier <u>Clemenceau,</u> flagship of the French Navy out of Marseilles. She was ordered to hunt down and destroy the terrorist boats.

The <u>Clemenceau</u> carried Super Etendard jet fighter-bombers, and Westland Lynx naval attack helicopters armed with AS12 anti-ship wire-guided missiles and 70mm rocket pods. Being the fastest `copters of their class, they could operate well ahead of their carrier, as could the Super Etendards which carried Exocet anti ship missiles. Within the hour, her jets had located the fast motor boats and destroyed them with cannon fire. A Lynx helicopter was despatched to recover Senior Sergeant Valery Stensis from the bemused Italians in Sardinia, and he very quickly identified the motor yacht which had quietly slipped out of Ajaccio in the confusion. A single AS 12 missile eliminated the need for arrest and trial. The Lynx returned him to his base at Calvi.

Chapter 4
ANALYSIS

Gil and Armentrude were advised that all flights from Ajaccio Aéroport Napoléon Bonaparte were cancelled due to the hostilities, so their departure was delayed. Shortly after that, They were arrested because someone had observed Gil shooting from their premises in the town during the terrorist attack. The Gendarmes delivered them to the fortress Head Quarters of the Foreign Legion, where they were brought before Commandant Victor Pintonen, and Senior Sergeant Valery Stensis, who commenced the interrogation.

"Mademoiselle Armentrude of Interpol Paris, and retired US Army Senior Sergeant Gilliemo Lamont, you are arrested on suspicion of breaching the security of a military operation. The situation is very grave . . . It is only because of your impeccable credentials, that we have convened this special enquiry. Interpol Paris have informed us of your complete backgrounds. We know you as well as you know yourselves. Do not try to evade our questions, or the consequences will be most severe".

Commandant Pintonen said nothing. Gil said nothing, but he identified Commandant Pintonen by the name above his seat in the Assembly Hall in which the enquiry was taking place.

"Senior Sergeant Lamont, please will you explain why you are in the company of an Interpol Agent, and apparently have her confidence, when your last employment was as a Motor Cycle Patrolman in Florida?"

Gil was experienced in this type of questioning, designed to un-settle the subject by revealing personal details, so he decided to try to defuse the strategy by a systematic attempt to disarm the questioner . . .

"Perhaps you are a little short sighted, or have you not noticed the very obvious charms of my lady companion".

"Do not trifle with me, Sergeant" . . .

"But that is the simple truth!" replied Gil, "please try to be more objective with your questions, and I am *not* a motorcycle cop, you should address me as Detective Sergeant" . . . . a long silence followed . . . Senior Sergeant Stensis looked rather tired.

"I am aware of your military career, and that you appear to have the backing of the highest authorities, but I need to know if there was any breach of security subsequent to my caution in the restaurant "Chez Doumé".

"Then I suggest that you identify and question that bespectacled and grey-haired man who was sitting in the restaurant that night" . . .

"We know that he is MI6, and beyond suspicion" . . .

"Really!", replied Gil sarcastically, "Do all Russians believe those devious Limies? I don`t know how your shaky security failed, but just may be, your battle plan was compromised by your opposing commander and his force without any leak in security".

At this, Commandant Pintonen interrupted . . .

"Enough Gentlemen! . . . Detective Sergeant Lamont, *now retired . . . we are not Russians!* Proud as we are of being eastern Europeans, we now serve France. Let us address the actual reason that you come before me . . . It seems that you fired shots with effect from the window of your premises, killing two and wounding another terrorist during the attack. For that, you gain our respect, but not our approval. Please explain why an un-armed tourist suddenly becomes a significant element in a serious fire-fight?"

"Quite simply Commandant, it may sound frivolous to you because of your perception of the "Hollywood" side of US culture, but where I come from it is considered right and proper to vanquish the bad guys by whatever means are available, whenever you find them. To my surprise, Mademoiselle Chemin produced her father's hunting rifle and it seemed opportune to use it. I hope that I was able to contribute just a little to enable the arrest of that boat and its crew by your off-duty men without further casualties. Should you need any further assistance, I am at your disposal" . . .

The hearing was suddenly interrupted by the entrance of the grey-haired man with spectacles . . .

"Oh bravo Sergeant . . . I have rarely heard such eloquence from an American, but be very careful what you are offering . . . tradition has it that once *in* the Legion, there is no possibility of resigning! I hope that you only intended to offer assistance in your present capacity *as a person on holiday*".

This surprise intervention succeeded in de-fusing the situation, and the Commandant summed-up the proceedings by saying, "It is concluded that sadly on this occasion, our attack was compromised by not engaging the enemy on land in Algeria, where our soldiers could be deployed with effect. The lack of an attack helicopter resulted in the loss of one Puma and damage to two others. In future, we will always fly with an escorting attack helicopter. This session is closed".

The grey-haired man with spectacles approached Gil and Armentrude and said quietly,

"Detective Sergeant Lamont, a quiet word if you please . . . and you Mademoiselle Chemin. Now that you are aware of my presence in my official capacity, perhaps we can co-exist and even co-operate in future, because frankly, I am instructed to arrange surveillance over you for the rest of your life . . . This will of course be discrete. It seems that you have somehow embarrassed some very distinguished persons. This action has also been approved by *your authorities* in the United States".

"Well I guess that kinda finalises the situation then", said Gil, "but I am in fact a free agent, not employed by any organisation, and I would like to stay that way. I normally don`t go out of my way to find trouble, and hope to live as quietly and comfortably as possible. However, should you wish to trace or to contact me, you can do that through Mademoiselle Armentrude in her official capacity".

Armentrude nodded her approval and said, "I . . . we have been recalled to Paris, and we will depart as soon as airline flights resume".

"Very well", replied the grey haired man, "if you are successful in retiring peacefully, we will not meet again, but I will know where you are and what you are doing".

Gil felt uncomfortable about that, feeling that this was the first obstacle before he had even started to find a quiet life.

The next morning they flew back to Paris, and Gil decided to try to write a book to give him something to do when Armentrude was at work.

At the fortress HQ of the Foreign Legion, a report on the final destruction of the terrorist force and the interrogation of the prisoners was sent to the French Government, and circulated to all interested parties. However, unknown to Commandant Pintonen, one of the escaping terrorist motor boats had paused to drop-off their Commander Abdul Salim in Sardinia, before resuming its course where it was sunk by the French Naval Etendards with the others. Salim was now free to contact hostile agents and to organise a reprisal to recover his reputation after defeat at Corsica, but this would take some time. His main advantage was that as far as he knew, no photograph of him had ever been published.He shaved off his beard anyway, and looked quite different, and found some suitable clothing on a washing line. He ate fruit and vegetables where he could find them, and black spiny sea urchins which required no cooking and were easily gathered from shallow sea water.He buried his old clothing, retaining his mobile `phone in a polythene bag for protection. He had no other possessions. He began to walk in search of Muslim brethren, heading towards Cagliari where he hoped to find a Mosque.

Chapter 5
THE QUIET LIFE

Gil took the opportunity to explore Paris. He visited the Louvre, took-in the view from the top of the Eiffel Tower, took a scenic boat trip on the Seine, and checked-out the Arc de Triomphe and Notre Dame. One Sunday with Armentrude, they visited Monet`s gardens at Givernie on the Seine. In the meantime he continued his attempt to put a book together, but boredom eventually won, and he began to think of fishing again . . . of Scotland`s Lochs and burns, of Steelheads in the Rockies, and the Everglades and Aluitious. One day when he was walking by the Seine, he suddenly noticed the un-mistakable head of Senior Sergeant Stensis walking ahead of him. It was raining, and the legionnaire was dressed in civilian clothes and wearing a grey raincoat, but his close-cut hair and sun-tanned scalp made him easy to spot in the Paris crowd.

Stensis paused at a news agent, and Gil deliberately brushed past him, turning to say,

"Oh pardon!", and then to pretend surprise at his recognition.

"Hey good buddy", said Gil, "you are a long way from base, what brings you to Paris?"

The apparently startled Sergeant composed himself and said, "perhaps we should talk somewhere less conspicuous".

Gil replied, "If being seen is that critical, perhaps you are right, but if our conversation is the problem, then the street is more secure".

"It is both I suppose, but I know a suitable café where we can talk discretely".

"Lead on", said Gil, all thoughts of fishing vanishing in an instant.

In the café, Stensis cautioned Gil, explaining that due to the special circumstances under which they had met in Corsica, he was extending a level of trust which was far beyond that which was normal between a US citizen and a Legionnaire from Eastern Europe.

Sensing the implied formality, and not wanting to get too involved in intrigue, Gil said,

"I don`t need any explanations. I really don`t mind why you are here . . . I don`t need to know. I was just surprised to see you here . . . a friend far from home".

"Nevertheless, you should realise that I have a sort of dual role in as much as I can relay certain intelligence between the Legion and those contacts in the old Eastern block".

"You are double agent then" . . . said Gil, "and you once threatened to kill me!".

"That remains a distant possibility", said Stensis, "but not one that I would relish. I hope that we can be useful to one another, should the occasion arise" . . .

Gil gave a resigned sigh . . . "I really *have* retired you know" . . .

But he said to himself, *I guess I deserved that if I am honest*, and to Stensis, "then why *are* you here?"

"We have decided to find out where exactly Al Qaeda get their Stingers and other high tech weapons from. We know that their small arms like Kalashnikovs and RPG`s come from Pakistan and Communist China via Syria and the Yemen, and enter Africa through the Sudan and Mogadishu, but the high tech weapons are not that simple to acquire. International arms dealers trade End User Certificates like Store Cards!". We suspect collusion at very high diplomatic levels, but are forbidden to investigate it. Instead we get "leaks" that enable us to intercept shipments en route, *after* the large suppliers and sometimes nations have made their profits. This high level `Sting` results in good publicity for the big players, East and West, but if it goes wrong, who knows where the weapons will end up? The Legion lost a Puma, six Legionnaires and two crew members in the last attack, so Commandant Pintonen plans to get even. But first we have to find out how the enemy got their missile". . .

Gil was silent for some time before replying. Then he said, "You stand a good chance of facing a Court Marshall if your suspicions are correct and you get found out . . . how did you intend to use *me*?"

"I don`t know yet, but as an ex army man, you are ideally qualified to work under-cover where I cannot . . . you have *all* the necessary contacts!".

`Don`t I just`, thought Gil, thinking of John Litton, Armentrude and her boss, Greenaway and the man with grey hair and spectacles.

"To obtain and export sophisticated ordnance such as missiles, it is necessary to have an End Users` Certificate. We believe that the type of shoulder-fired missile which brought down our Puma came from manufacturers in Eastern Europe . . . possibly the Czech Republic or Russia.

Without this Certificate, moving it across borders would be very difficult. Of course, illegal drops from aircraft can and do take place across once Communist-controlled airspace into the Middle-East and Asia, but this has become more unlikely due to the presence of U.S. Forces in Afghanistan and Turkey and their surveillance activities. We think that the weapons travel overland to the northeast Mediterranean, where large motor yachts collect them. To cover-up their sale to dissident groups, a falsified End User Certificate is raised here in Paris by dissident sympathisers, and smuggled back to the manufacturers to show that the weapons were issued to their own military or some other legal destination" . . . Stensis paused to allow this information to sink-in. "I am here to investigate this, but I am too obvious. I was thinking that you could help here by following a known suspect to see how he collects the false End User Certificate, and who from".

"You make it sound like you intended us to meet! . . . I thought that I was following you", said Gil.

"Well we knew that you and your companion live here, and your address, but we would prefer that Interpol and the other Official Services were not informed should you decide to assist us. We will cover all expenses and provide more money if you are successful".

"How much more money?" asked Gil cautiously.

"Enough!", said Stensis. "Here is how to contact me . . . think about it", and handing Gil a card he got up and left, leaving Gil to pay the bill.

Gil did not like the idea of keeping secrets from Armentrude, but the truth was that he was becoming bored. He paid the bill, and went home to prepare the supper.

In Sardinia, a weary Abdul Salim was still walking south towards Cagliari where he hoped to find Muslim sympathisers who by tradition would feed and assist him. On the fourth day he reached the outskirts of the Sardinian Capital. He paused for a cup of tea at a transport café, and the friendly Italian owner regaled him with his experiences in North Africa during World War 2.

"Is there a Mosque in Cagliari?", asked Salim.

"Yes there is, we have all a man could desire here, but it is some distance. Too far to walk on a hot day, especially during siesta. Have some more apple tea".

"Thank you no, but perhaps you might know the address, or some directions" said Salim, rising to leave.

"It is in the Via del Collega, a rather dilapidated area of Cagliari", said the Italian, but my friend Alphonso drives past every afternoon, and will give you a lift if you stay for a while and have some more tea". So Abdul Salim had more tea, and waited for his lift.

Chapter 6
INEVITABLE INVOLVEMENT

Gil thought long and hard about Senior Sergeant Stensis` offer. He hated the prospect of hiding anything from Armentrude, but he did not want to put her career at risk. In the end, his professional instinct prevailed and he contacted Stensis, accepting his offer of investigating the shady world of weapon sales . . . modern gun-runners.

Stensis arranged to meet Gil beside the Seine whenever they wished to exchange information regarding targets for observation. Any non-critical conversations or instructions could be passed by cell phone. At one such meeting, Stensis pointed out a short middle-aged man with a receding hairline in a grey suit, and asked Gil to follow him and to report if he did anything which might prove to be an exchange or pick-up of documents.

Gil followed the man who Stensis said was a suspected link in the illegal export of weapons. He took the Metro from Pont Neuf near Notre Dame towards Le Bois de Vincennes. The carriage was not crowded that afternoon, and the man was sitting reading a magazine. The underground train stopped at Quai de la Rapée, and another passenger in jeans and bomber jacket brushed past him and deftly placed an envelope on the open magazine which the suspect immediately closed and put in his brief case. The man in the bomber jacket got off the train. Gil`s cell phone was screened while on the underground, so he could not advise Stensis. At Faidherbe-Chaligny the suspect got off. Gil followed him up onto the Rue de Montreuil, and reporting their position to Stensis, continued to follow him.

Eventually the suspect entered a building on the Rue Faidherbe, and Gil chose a position from which he could observe the front of the building without being seen, and waited for instructions. It began to rain, and he was getting very uncomfortable when Stensis came quietly up the street in a Citroen C3 . . . Gil got in.

"Damn rain,I hope you make this worthwhile . . . I could be on a beach in Calvi", said Gil.

Stensis just grunted . . . Just then the suspect came out of the front door and walked away from them up the street.

"Wait until he reaches that side turning, and then we will jump him. We will make it look like a mugging, and will leave him unconscious. If he does not have the envelope on him, we will take his keys and gain entry to that building!", said Stensis.

"We? . . . I`ll wait outside with the car . . . I don`t want to be involved in mugging or illegal entry", said Gil.

"Too late to discuss it now" said Stensis, and accelerating up to the Suspect, swerved across the road, jumped out and pushed the suspect into the side road where he rendered him unconscious, took his wallet and some keys, leaving him on the ground.

Back in the car, he passed the wallet to Gil, and drove back to the house. Gil found seventy-five Euros, a business card from a Samir Kahn, manager of a small firm which printed labels and time-tables, but no other ID. Stensis stopped outside the house. It was now getting dark, and no lights showed . . .

"Did you see anyone else go in or come out?", he asked.

"No", said Gil.

Stensis jumped out again, saying "you drive now . . . be ready for a quick get-away". With that he used the keys to open the door, and entered the house. He came out after a few minutes with the brief case, and said "hit it!" . . .

Gil needed no encouragement, and as they drove smartly away, asked "where to now?"

"First, dump these keys near our unconscious friend, and then back to the centre of town and find a car park where we will ditch the car", said Stensis . . .

"Where did you get it?", asked Gil.

"I stole it", said Stensis, without a flicker of guilt . . . "it will be found and returned to its owner".

"Oh that's all right then!", said Gil sarcastically, "I guess it's time for my supper now, I'll drive home, and *you* can ditch the car. I don't know how much my contribution to this crime was worth, but it had better be good if you expect me to do any more". . .

Stensis was checking the brief case . . . "We hit gold", he said, "in the magazine there are two documents. One is the End User Certificate, the other concerns something called 'Genetic manipulation by DNA Synthesis and Nano-carriers' . . . I'll burn that".

"The hell you will!" . . . Gil was suddenly all attention, "that could be worth more than thousands of missiles you dummy, give it to me!"

"What will *you* do with it without revealing how you obtained it?" demanded Stensis.

Gil sighed . . . "I guess we will have to come clean, but don`t mention stealing the car, or the mugging. Just say that you were on a covert mission and obtained these documents from a certain premises. Ditch the car, and stay with me and Armentrude tonight. Tomorrow we will all go to Interpol and tell them only what they need to know, and hand over the documents".

"But I am expected to send the certificate to my handler in Eastern Europe".

"We`ll email them a copy and the name and address of the printer Samir Kahn, but omit to tell them that Interpol know. They will all find out eventually. It is a fair bet that the guy in the bomber jacket is Samir Kahn".

"He is a minor player, I am not interested in him. He may be a sympathiser, or he may not even know what an End User Certificate is. He is just a printer".

After dropping off Gil, he drove off to get rid of the car, returning after about forty five minutes to stay with Gil and Armentrude, who was initially delighted to see him, but her suspicions were aroused when Gil explained that Valery Stensis was here on a covert mission, and had recovered evidence of illegal arms trading.

"We will go to Interpol in the morning where all will be revealed", said Gil in an attempt to re-assure her, but she remained quite composed anyway, confident that provided that she kept her Section Chief informed, these two extraordinary men could not compromise her.

Chapter 7
A QUESTION OF CONTROL

That night, the three comrades endured a tortuous discussion with some dispute over the involvement of Special Sergeant Valery Stensis. His Commanding Officer apparently believed that his Sergeant was on leave to visit Latvia. His covert handler in Eastern Europe was not aware of Gil`s involvement in the recovery of the documents, or that they were staying with an Interpol Agent. Of course, it was agreed that Stensis` role as a double agent would not be disclosed to Interpol, but Armentrude said that they already knew because Gil had told her and she had already reported it. Stensis was not pleased . . .

Eventually, they agreed that in Paris they would all act as free independent agents, co-operating as much as possible without compromising each other further. In Corsica, if they returned, or anywhere else when working with the French Foreign Legion, Stensis would be in control. Gil said that all he wanted was a quiet life, but even he did not really believe that. His die was cast the moment he had joined the MCIS. He could not help himself.

In NORAD, the White House, Interpol, and at GCHQ, the implied threat of genetically modified bio-weapons, together with the potential of applied nanotechnology was viewed with grave despondence. The problem was that now that Osama Bin Laden was dead, who was the controlling mind behind Al Qaeda's campaign? In which country did he or she reside? Did any current terrorist organisation have the technology to manufacture and to deliver such weapons? What was the view of Russia and Communist China regarding these weapons in terrorist hands?

Did North Korea have any involvement, or was it simply a few deranged Muslims with a lot of money? Western society had long accepted Islam as being a major player amongst world religions in contributing towards modern civilisation, but was persistently confounded by acts of violence by terrorists claiming motivation from verses in the Holy Koran. A view vigorously denied by Imams worldwide.

In the Mosque at the city of Cagliari in Sardinia, Abdul Salim was of course welcomed initially, but his hosts became uneasy when he referred to the attacks in Corsica with no sympathy for the innocent civilians killed and wounded. He spent many hours talking with contacts in the Middle East on his mobile `phone. After a few days, they hoped he would leave them as soon as possible. Eventually, money arrived and he departed by ferry to the Italian mainland. When he was certain that Abdul Salim was safely away on the ferry, the Imam dutifully informed the Carabineri that a strange traveller had stayed with them. This information disappeared into the Italian Police records where things could remain un-disturbed for scores of years.

High over the Arctic, Mil-sat 114 was adjusting its orbit and altitude, responding to signals from Gold Hill Airforce Base, Alaska. Its new mission was to get images of an installation in North Africa which had been recently constructed by a Chino-Arabic consortium. It was hoped that the purpose of this industrial centre could be deduced from these pictures.

In London, Giles Greenaway had just arrived at Northolt in his Gulfstream 3000. He was due to attend a meeting of the Hadley Frobisher Committee for Policy Review, an august body of specialists who made recommendations to HMG. They were awaiting the interpretation of satellite images and other data from which they could draw sufficient conclusions to advise whether the new facility constituted a threat. Enquiries through diplomatic channels had revealed that the buildings in North Africa were for the manufacture of badly needed medicines. The remote position of the facility threw grave doubt as to the veracity of this claim, especially since there was insufficient natural water in that zone for industrial scale production of medicines.

As his driver headed towards Whitehall, he mused over the circumstances surrounding the recovery of this data. The concern about the new buildings in North Africa had been kick-started by reports from Interpol. The aspect which Giles found irritating was the resurgence of the name Gil Lamont . . . His name cropped-up in the Interpol Report, and also in the Special Surveillance Report, an internal Ministry of Defence document. Giles had instigated a trace on Lamont as a precaution when he had been embarrassed during the Luccombe fiasco, but Giles never imagined that this relatively unimportant American would be involved in matters of International Security. *What an extraordinary man this chap was!*

Giles was uneasy about the apparent liaison between the undercover agent allocated to monitor Lamont's activities and the subject himself. He resigned himself to accept that the name Gil Lamont would probably recur again. This man seemed to forestall trouble ; he had a remarkable tenacity, and an ability to identify where it might occur. His MI6 agent had reported that Lamont was back in Paris, but that he had already been involved in the recovery of forged End User Certificates and data concerning the production of genetically modified organisms and their possible use as a weapon of mass destruction . . . Bio-weapons. The United Nations had not yet come to terms with the use of Chemical weapons, let alone shown any consideration regarding a policy in the event that Bio-weapons were used.

In the conference room at Whitehall, the scientists on the Hadley Frobisher Committee explained that the problem with a biological attack was that it could be masked as a natural outbreak of disease due to factors such as climate change and/or pollution by agricultural biocides. Most reagents were undetectable at airports by current technology. The vector could be introduced into public water supplies in small quantities such that initially only a few persons were affected, but within whom disease would rapidly develop and spread to Pandemic levels. The threat was very real, and there was a strong suspicion in some quarters that the successive outbreaks of cattle diseases such as *Foot and Mouth, Bovine Encephalitis, Tuberculosis, Blue Tongue, and even Brucellosis* in recent years had been deliberately introduced by subversive elements to develop the procedure.

Meanwhile, in Wyoming the Homeland Defence Committee comprising an Admiral and a senior Commander from the US Marines, an Army General and an Airforce General, with a representative from the Office of the Secretary of State, and scientists from NASA, Woods Hole, JPL and MIT were nervously awaiting the arrival of the President at their underground communications centre.

Chairman Admiral Walter Revere USN, put down his telephone and said,

"All rise for the Commander in Chief, gentlemen", and they all stood up.

The door opened and an Aid entered announcing, "Gentlemen, the President of the United States".

All present stood at attention.

"Please be seated gentlemen", said the President taking the Chair, "Now what's all this about? . . . to be frank, we have been here before!" . . .

"Well yes Mr. president, in 2001 we destroyed what was claimed to be an "Aspirin factory" for the same reason as now, but despite international dismay we believe that your predecessor was correct, resulting in a setback of some eight or nine years for those who want to use bio-weapons".

"Let's get right to the point, and I want strait answers . . . If I sanction a cruise missile attack, what are the chances of collateral damage?"

"None Mr. President, the facility is too remote", said Admiral Revere.

"Is that the opinion of you all?

"Yes Mr. President, it is", replied the Admiral.

"What if some of the bio-agent escaped and blew downwind?"

"We believe that there is little risk, because the live substance is unlikely to survive in the very dry and extreme temperatures of the Sahara Desert".

"But some of the personnel present may become infected. Could they escape and spread the disease?"

"As you can see on this screen Mr. President, we will be observing, and if necessary we can send a drone to eliminate each and every one".

"Very well gentlemen . . . go do it! . . . but not before we have advised the United Nations that we have identified a real threat to Nations of the Free World, and we will not hesitate to eliminate it for the good of every human being".

The President stood up, wished them all success in their work, and left the room as quickly as he had arrived.

Chapter 8
PREVENTION IS BETTER THAN CURE...

After attending the meeting of the Hadleigh Frobisher Committee, Giles Greenaway was even more worried than usual. This chap Gil Lamont had hit the jackpot again. His name had come up during the conference, and questions had been asked about his qualifications.

Was he qualified to make such important judgements about the importance of DNA Synthesis and bio-weapons? asked some of the professors. What did he know about nano-technology?. The Chairman, Lord Skidestie drily pointed out that qualified or not, when it came to a vital judgement call, he had made the right one! Furthermore, he believed that he had briefly met Lamont during a fishing holiday at Castle Kerreg in Scotland, and found him to be a sound fellow.

"Very few people, including *ourselves*, are qualified in this obscure subject, so don`t waste valuable time with such pointless nonsense when so much is at stake", he had rebuked them.

The mention of Gil Lamont at Castle Kerreg was quite alarming to Giles. His association with the whole episode, if revealed could do him irreparable damage. Now Lamont had intruded into his world again, still holding the high moral ground.

Giles had come away from the meeting actioned to investigate all possible means of frustrating the manufacture and distribution of chemical and bio-weapons, their methods of delivery, and probable targets.

"Well they say that if you can't beat them, *use them!*", he said out loud. He spent the next several hours thinking how he might use Lamont in the most dangerous assignments, keeping him too busy to reveal their association. Perhaps he might also become a casualty.

Meanwhile, Abdul Salim had rejoined his contacts in Rafah in the Gaza Strip, on the border with Egypt. Here, the leaders of Hezbollah, Al Qaeda, and the Arab Spring held planning meetings in which they identified highly qualified Muslim sympathisers in universities and industry world-wide. These specialised scientists and engineers were lavishly entertained in places like Abu Dhabi and Doha, where they were offered generous funding, ostensibly for humanitarian research projects in South East Asia. The hidden agenda was to tap their expertise for application in the production of chemical, biological and nuclear weapons for use against the very countries in which they had the freedom to work. In a few cases it might prove possible to "turn" these experts and get their full-time co-operation in the business of death and destruction for the infidel.

One of the key documents to be used in the co-ordination of this had mysteriously gone missing in Paris, after one of their agents was mugged. Abdul Salim and his associates were unsure whether the two events were linked, because the agent did not have the document on him when he was mugged.

While still "on leave" from the Foreign Legion, Senior Sergeant Stensis travelled to the manufacturer of the Stinger type man-portable anti-aircraft weapon in the Check Republic.

With their co-operation, he arranged for a missile to be bugged with a signal transmitter which was initiated whenever it came close to an electromagnetic source greater than 0.3 micro-farads. This very faint signal could be detected by military satellites which had been programmed to search for it. The missile would also fail to respond to guidance system commands, should it be launched. Since these were "Point and fire" type missiles, it was unlikely that the user would detect these modifications before use. It was then sent to the despatch department complete with the forged End User Certificate. Senior Sergeant Stensis returned to his base at Calvi where he reported to Commandant Pintonen that he had had a very enjoyable visit to his relatives in Latvia.

Homeland Security Specialists in Wyoming USA, GCHQ and Scotland Yard in England, C-in-C NATO in Brussels, and Interpol in Paris, studied the situation and decided to wait in the hope of getting United Nations approval to take out the facility in Southern Sahara. However, they only had to programme and switch-on their Satellite to see where the missile was sent. Now in each of these centres, screens were switched on and down-links established. Watches were kept at all centres, and gradually, signals emerged in the most unexpected places, indicating that the missile was travelling by road initially, the signal appearing whenever the vehicle passed beneath or over power cables. It spent a night in a refrigeration plant, and next morning a strong and continuous signal was received when it travelled by rail on an electrified route. To everyone`s surprise, it eventually arrived at Tablisi on the Black Sea coast of Georgia after about a week. From there it was flown to Qatar, and on to Sanaa in the Yemen. This raised concern that once clear of the airport and town, transport may be by mule or camel, and tracking would be lost.It was decided that special forces should be tasked with identifying and eliminating the End Users as soon as possible. Requests were put to each centre.

Since Senior Sergeant Stensis had been involved, Interpol put his name forward without hesitation. NATO looked towards the UK and the SAS, and Giles Greenaway suggested that Detective Sergeant Gil Lamont should represent the United States for the same reason. Homeland Security agreed, and Gil received movement orders to report to Toulouse within 24 hours. Armentrude was amazed and at the same time dismayed.

The team assembled in the Sofitel at 14.00 hrs. local time the next day. A Royal Airforce C130 Hercules had arrived at Blagnac with all the necessary equipment, an Officer in charge of the Operations Communication Centre in an all-terrain vehicle, a Lieutenant who was referred to as Mike and two other ranks, all SAS. The C130 was directed to an empty hangar at the "old" part of the airfield, St. Martin, where they were joined by Sergeants Stensis and Lamont, and a Belgian soldier.

The SAS men greeted them informally . . .

"Listen up guys, my name is Mike, and this is Boss, our Ops Base Comms Captain. We have the pleasure of the company of Jim and Bill, our weapons and explosives specialists. I understand that you are Sergeants Valery and

Gil, accompanied by Nicholas or Nick from Belgium. We have brought a formidable armoury with us, and I want you all to spend the next hour familiarising yourselves with all the equipment, especially the comms sets. I take it that you are used to using night vision gear".

Nick the Belgian painted a Badger on the side of the special vehicle, and they began to call it "The Badger", an armoured six-wheeled vehicle with a turret-mounted heavy machine gun. It had a range of about a thousand miles with additional fuel cans carried externally, depending on the terrain.

To his surprise, Gil found himself fitting in like a duck to water, he just liked these guys and the professional way they all got stuck-in. He realised how much he missed the service life. *Outstanding*, he thought to himself, and then, *I must be off my and trolley to get involved with these guys, I am supposed to be retired!*

Lt. Mike approached Gil and said, "Sergeant Lamont, may I call you Gil?"

Gil nodded. Mike continued, "you were specially recommended by the MOD as a person with exceptional ability. They did not elaborate, but you must have impressed some very important people. Welcome to our little group. I have seen your service record and know that you will be a useful addition. The rest of us have worked together on several ops. and we each know our roles. Nick the Belgian is our "up-close and personal silent killer". I will on occasion consult you, but the rest of us are just ordinary soldiers".

A likely story! thought Gil, *they look older than ordinary grunts. Also he has met Valery Stensis before.*

Gil said to Stensis, "you know these guys then!"

Stensis replied, "Yes, when we first met, in 1967, I was on the other side . . . that is why they call me Stazi."

Oh boy! thought Gil grimly, *we got hundreds of man-years of violence and unpleasant experience here.*

At 23.00 hrs. the group was ordered to move complete with Ops Base to RAF Akrotiri in Cypress, and they all boarded the C130 for the flight to the far end of the Mediterranean.

Gil asked if he could use his mobile `phone during the flight.

Mike said "yes at this time".

So despite the noise of the aircraft, Gil rang Armentrude.

"We are flying to Cypress on vacation", said Gil.

"I know, I am watching you Cheri, I cannot say more now!"

Gil realised the significance of her reply, and said "OK, love you", and rang off.

After a flight of some seven hours from Toulouse, they landed at RAF Akrotiri in Cyprus, with orders to standby . . . The local time was 08.30 hrs. and despite it being daylight, Mike ordered the loading ramp and aircraft doors shut, hammocks to be rigged, and all members of the battle group to sleep for at least five hours if the tactical situation did not require further action. No more personal telephone calls allowed.

In Wyoming, the Duty Officer and his team of analysts noted the signal from the missile was moving sporadically towards the coast, finally arriving at Turbah, a fishing village and nearest point to the Eritrean coast of Africa after two more days.

Admiral Revere's committee deliberated over its final destination, and how it might be used. What was its target, and how could a single Stinger missile with very limited range and which could only destroy one aircraft, be of any tactical or strategic use?

They were quite certain that its role was not connected in any way to the existence of the suspected Chemical and Biological facility, nearly a thousand miles away in Sub-Saharan Africa. They therefore passed the responsibility for any tactical decisions to the Special Forces Group on the ground, but would continue to advise on the location of the missile.

It was no surprise when the signal next appeared in Djibouti, and finally in Bandar Cassim in northern Somalia.

In Cyprus, the Boss and Mike decided that it was time to move closer to the End Users. They now believed that the missile might be used to attack one of the helicopters deployed by NATO patrol vessels who were trying to suppress piracy between the Gulf of Aqaba and Mogadishu. A decision was approved for them to move to HMS Tarantula, a Royal Navy Assault Vessel which they would join at Aden. The Tarantula and HMS Mountbatten were currently on station in the area with similar elements of the Dutch and US Navies.

Accordingly, their C130 flew the Group and all its equipment to Aden, before returning to RAF Lyneham.

Now on board the Tarantula, the Special Forces Group had time to relax and train with the Royal Marines who were the normal complement of this massive Assault vessel. Gil was frankly surprised at the fire power of this ship. He had been to sea with the US Navy in the South

China sea, but found the Royal Navy traditions and formalities different but quite easy to comply with. Their patrol took them down the Coast of Somalia, some 200 miles off-shore.

On the fourth day, a call for assistance was received from a 300 thousand ton tanker out of Hamburg. The German reported three fast motor gun boats shadowing them. They were ninety miles to the south west. HMS Mountbatten was south of the targets, distant some three hours steaming time. She despatched her Lynx Helicopter and sank two of the three pirate boats, but the third moved away to the north, where she was run down by HMS Tarantula. The Royal Marines picked-up two survivors for interrogation.

Mike, Stensis and Gil were allowed to interview the captured pirates in the presence of the ship`s First Officer. Since the NATO Patrol did not have a UN mandate to hold prisoners, it was inevitable that they would be released with a "caution". However, these men were uneducated village fishermen who had found a more lucrative way of making a living, so they were told that they would only be released on condition that they answered all the questions put to them. Stensis and Gil wanted to know if these pirates knew anything about the use of the Stinger Missile, but they had great difficulty understanding the frightened prisoners. Eventually, a Tarantula crew member who had spent time in Somalia was summoned. He was a natural story teller, and wove a terrifying tale about the prisoners` fate if they did not co-operate. Eventually, it emerged that Arabs had come to their village with tales of a magic weapon which could destroy the helicopters, but the prisoners had seen no sign of one yet. The Arabs had instructed them to concentrate on oil tankers rather than smaller vessels and yachts. The pirates were promised generous payments in return.

The Tarantula now made for Mogadishu, where the prisoners were to be handed over to the authorities. The Special Forces Group were landed after dark with all their equipment in the special all-terrain vehicle with satellite communications.

Chapter 9
THE CURE...

During the interrogation of the captured pirates, it was determined that most of the pirate motor boats came from the coast to the north east of Mogadishu, where the Horn of Africa was closest to the trade routes from the Gulf Ports to the rest of the world. The Special Forces Group drove 750 miles north to Qardho, a small town through which any land transport would most likely pass to reach the coast. The landscape was dry and brown, and Gil could not imagine how anyone could survive here, let alone want to. Occasionally they passed very shallow lakes which were fed by dry waterways, but there was no agriculture, and no green vegetation. Twice they replenished their water supplies filling empty fuel cans for use should they run short of drinking water. Being contaminated with diesel, this could be passed through a filtration system until it was safe to drink, but still smelled and tasted of fuel.

After three days of hard driving, they stopped for a tactical review just short of the town. The vehicle with Boss and the Comms centre were concealed beneath camouflage nets some distance off the track.

The rest of the group took up positions to spot the enemy as they approached. They were in continuous radio contact with Boss and each other on an open channel. The Satellite tracker reported that the missile and its party was last located some ten klicks north north west of their position, and Boss was worried that they may have passed or evaded the group. They had passed some local people on the track, who may have been able to report their presence that afternoon.

"They may look primitive, but don`t underestimate them" he said.

Gil who was on high ground spotted and reported three armed men moving up a waddy and concealed from Jim and Bill close by. The three men were clearly searching, and cautiously dispersed towards higher ground, but in so doing, two were heading towards Mike and Nick the Belgian.

Mike alerted the group for action, saying, "Jim, stay concealed and challenge them to halt, lower their weapons and raise their hands for questioning. Use English, Italian and French".

Before he had finished the Italian challenge, two of the men ran towards Mike and Nick, the other took cover without moving very far.

Mike shot both his targets, killing the first and wounding the second. Nick put this man out of his agony.

Bill gave a burst from his nine millimetre automatic close to the third man who stood up, hands raised. The group now approached him from all sides, but he drew a hand gun and waved it about hysterically. Mike killed him with a single pistol shot. They recovered the small arms and buried the bodies.

"We must assume that our presence here is detected, leaving us no option but to locate their main party with a view to eliminating them and the missile as the End Users.

It will be dark soon which will give us the advantage", said Mike.

They returned to Boss and Badger, the vehicle.

Boss reported the missile as being at the coast, so they packed up and proceeded down the track towards Bandarbeyla where the tracking signal had given a very weak indication.

Within two klicks, a rocket-propelled grenade was fired at the vehicle being driven by Bill who swerved, yelling "Incoming!"

Mike, who was riding "watch" on top of the vehicle was cut and scorched by the blast and debris as it exploded on the left side of the track. He returned automatic fire with the heavy machine gun, targeting a ridge some 800 metres away. There was no return fire from the ridge.

Night vision head sets enabled them to cover the next 100 miles to a village called Dudo before daybreak. Now they were only about 60 road miles from their destination. They paused to check for signs of hostiles, before driving through the village at full speed with no opposition, scattering dogs, chickens and the odd pig in a cloud of dust as they disappeared into the rising sun.

Two hours later found them on high ground overlooking the Indian Ocean, an enticing blue in contrast to the sun scorched land through which they had been driving. From here they could see the fishing village with boats pulled up clear of the ocean swells which seemed to emerge from an otherwise calm sea. A three ton truck and a four wheel drive civilian vehicle were clearly visible, but very few people were out in the open because the sun was now very hot, giving an air temperature of 47 degrees Centigrade. To approach the village without detection was almost impossible. The road now snaked down the steep escarpment with hairpin bends. Any attempt to drive down would raise clouds of dust, and the speed at the bends would be so slow that they would be sitting ducks. They pushed the Badger off the track, concealing it as well as they could beneath camouflage nets amongst the rocky outcrops and awaited darkness, nearly ten hours away.

Mike set Jim on the first two hour watch, and the rest of them needed no encouragement to try to sleep. Hot tea and tinned rations were served between watches, as the day dragged on. Gil longed to dive into the ocean, and dreamed of those lazy days with Armentrude in Corsica. If the enemy knew how close they were, they showed no sign of it. In the late afternoon, two fast motor boats came in, and were met by a dozen men who pulled them clear of the surf. An hour later, a larger boat came in and anchored about five hundred yards offshore.

Mike briefed the group, saying that their objective was to destroy the End Users rather than the missile which was known to be useless anyway. The object of hostilities being to demonstrate to Somali pirates and supporting Arab terrorists that the acquisition and use of high tech weapons was impractical, and not worth the severe punishment. In such primitive circumstances, the End Users were those in charge of the truck and the four wheel drive vehicle, plus anyone associating with them as well as the motor boats and their crews. The group would attack an hour after sunset when it was sufficiently dark, leaving Boss and the Comms in Badger, the Assault vehicle concealed where it was. He was to alert them if any hostiles appeared from inland behind them. The total number of hostiles was unknown, but the intention after eliminating them was to secure the village and to call HMS Tarantula to collect the group complete with Boss and the Badger Armored Personnel Carrier.

Just before dark Nick the Belgian who was on watch reported that one of the motor boats was being launched, and the missile was being loaded onto it, presumably for transfer to the vessel anchored offshore. The Tarantula was informed that they were about to engage the End Users, and that the missile was being transferred to the larger pirate motor vessel.

Mike said, "Let it go . . . we won`t move until it is truly dark. It will be a good thing if they fire the missile at a chopper, because it *will* miss, and they will get sunk. If any survive, they will report that the missile was no damn good!"

Meanwhile, Boss went back behind their position and placed battery-operated movement detectors in a wide arc to provide a warning of hostile approach from the rear.

Half an hour later, they began to descend the rocky escarpment armed with grenade launchers, 9mm Hecla and Cock automatic weapons and Glock hand guns. Boss watched from the top of the escarpment, armed with a sniper rifle. Mike lead from the centre with Gil to his left and Jim out beyond him at left wing. On his right was Stensis and Bill with Nick at right wing. They advanced quietly down towards the village in a line,with about fifty metres between them.They all had head sets with night vision and an open channel to Boss and each other. Less than a hundred metres from the main village there were some lean-to sheds for goats and a couple of donkeys.

Taking cover behind these enclosures, Mike said, "I will open fire with two RPG`s, taking out both vehicles. This will bring out all the hostiles inside the buildings, but take out those already outside first, and then the rest. Destroy all motor boats within range and any fuel, weapons and ammunition. We will then take and hold the village. At this time, Boss will contact HMS Tarantula and advise them that we are engaging the target and will require a landing craft to transfer us complete with our vehicle back on board, and we can all go home. Are you ready gentlemen? . . . Jim?"

"Yo".

"Gil?"

"I`m Good".

"Stazi?"

"Oui".

"Bill?"

"Yes".

"Nick?"

"Ya", said Nick, and Mike opened fire.

The four wheel drive vehicle split open like a can, its fuel burning and exploding containers of RPG`s and other ammunition which had been within it. The truck just fell in half. All hostiles already outside were taken out, but to everyones` annoyance, none emerged from the buildings in which they were known to be. Nick fired another RPG into the largest building, and its roof collapsed at one end, with flames emerging from every aperture. Jim who was closest fired another at the second building which clearly held fuel, as it erupted like a volcano and disappeared. Now they advanced into the village, but as soon as they broke cover, bursts of automatic fire came from one end of the large burning building. All of the group dived for cover and engaged it with their Hecla and Cock weapons. Jim reported that he was winded by a round in his Kevla vest, but still shooting.

Bill worked his way round cover to flank the hostile(s) who were still returning fire, and inserted a small package into the building which then collapsed with a dull bang, followed by silence only broken by the sound of howling dogs, and crying children in the rest of the village. The smell of burnt cordite was stinging their throats, and the village smell was not too good either.

At this point, all heard the movement detector warning over their headsets, and Boss reported that he had returned to the Badger. Now Mike and Gil were cautiously checking out the remains of the buildings, and confirmed no survivors. Gil picked-up as many documents as he could find which had not yet caught alight, and they then regrouped outside, all taking cover within the village.

Boss began to contact HMS Tarantula, but was forced to lay down suppressing fire to the rear with the heavy machine gun. An incoming RPG was fortunately hit and destroyed in flight by a heavy burst from this 70mm weapon. Small arms fire was now hitting the vehicle and Boss was forced to break out from his camouflage net and semi-concealed position, but his view from the driver's position was partially obscured be the trailing net. He could not see the track, and the vehicle careered down the escarpment into the village, bursting through several ramshackle buildings. The externally stowed Gerry cans full of water were taking most of the incoming hits, but there was no good cover for the Badger whose massive foam-filled tyres were now shredded by bullets and the rough terrain, resulting in serious loss of speed and agility. Inside, Boss heard that the Tarantula had despatched a Lynx, which fortunately arrived overhead within minutes. Boss requested suppression on the top of the escarpment.

The Lynx crew replied. "roger that", and 70 mm rockets lit up a thirty metre strip at the top where they could see hostiles firing. Now the whole area was quiet, and any remaining hostiles had vanished into the darkness but the sound of a motor boat engine alerted the group, and looking seawards they saw tracer incoming from beyond the range of their small arms.

Back in the Badger, Boss manned the 70mm Machine gun and returned fire, and the Lynx followed suit, but the larger motor boat fired the dud missile at it. The weapon shot strait up and after a few seconds, its solid fuel rocket motor exhausted, it fell harmlessly into the sea. Now the Lynx sunk the remaining motor boats with its machine gun and 70mm rocket pods.

Mike posted Nick, Stensis and Gil as sentries, while he checked out Jim who had a couple of broken ribs beneath his Kevlar vest. Within the hour, a Landing craft arrived from the Tarantula, and the damaged Badger complete with Boss and all the group, embarked for the trip out to the Tarantula on the horizon. Gil was impressed when the stern of the enormous grey vessel opened, and the landing craft sailed right on in, to dock in the bowels of the ship. Within minutes, Jim was in the surgery, and the rest got hot showers and clean uniforms.

Back in Paris, it was still only early evening, and Armentrude was at home feeling lonely and worried, when the phone rang. It was Gil, saying the he would hopefully soon be home, and that he loved her. She felt as if an enormous weight had been lifted from her head and shoulders.

Within a week, Stensis was back in Calvi, Gil was in Paris, the SAS were in Herefordshire and Nick the Belgian was at home in Brussels.

Armentrude pleaded with Gil not to go on any more operations.

Gil replied, "I guess in my business, you don`t get a choice".

In London, the Hadleigh Frobisher Committee were delighted with the outcome of the Joint Special Forces Group`s operation to track down and destroy those involved in the illegal distribution of high tech weapons. The documents recovered by Gil Lamont from the building destroyed in Somalia had revealed a link to an Abdul Salim of Al Qaeda and Hezbollah in the Gaza Strip, and had also been circulated to the new industrial complex in Sub-Saharan Africa. Information so far received enhanced their suspicions that the facility was a laboratory for the development of Chemical and Bio Weapons, which when combined with nano-technology delivery systems required very little volume to achieve devastating damage. Such small quantities required very little water during preparation, and hence could be produced in remote arid areas, unlike industrial production of medicines.

At the White House, the President was briefed by the Chiefs of staff of the armed services.

As Commander-in-Chief, he had the authority to order the launch of cruise missiles at the enemies of the United States, but his dilemma was that these buildings in Africa were not in themselves a demonstrable threat to the USA. It seemed prudent to discuss the situation with the

United Nations' Security Council first, and then to put it to the vote in Congress.

In Great Britain, the Prime Minister was in a very similar position, but was well aware that the House of Commons was unlikely to agree to the use of cruise missiles to attack a threat which as yet had not materialised.

The world's press exploded with every possible uninformed argument. Russia and China vetoed all resolutions put before the United Nations.

Chapter 10
"OUR SOLUTION IS AT HAND"

Meanwhile, a Joint African Defence Force, organised by the nations of Africa to use their standing armies to combat colonialism and assist each other when necessary, had been mobilised comprising the Algerian Army with support from Kenya, Zambia and Nigeria. Encouraged by its recent operation to liberate the BP Oil Pumping Station, this Task Force requested technical support from the United Nations in order to assist in the suppression of the Ganjaweed terrorist gangs in the Southern Sahara. The United Nations granted approval and recommended advisors from special forces in the United States, France and the UK.

These specialists were contacted as individuals by the Algerian Army, and asked if they would assist in a technical capacity only. Their advice was sought regarding the most effective way to locate known Ganjaweed bases, but the modus operandi of the gangs was such that they had no permanent bases. Those specialists that responded travelled as civilians to a meeting in Malta, to discuss the mission, its objectives, and how they might be resolved. Despite their precautions, this did not go un-noticed by security organisations in the United States, France and UK.

At a secret meeting in the Bahamas between Admiral Walter Revere USN, US Army General Sherman Blund, FFL Commandant Victor Pintonen, and Giles Greenaway, it was agreed that in this sensitive situation, it would be prudent to consider the possibility of covert support of the African forces by certain specialists familiar with this area of operation, some of whom had recently visited Malta. This would most probably provide an opportunity to get close to the target buildings which were near Kichi Kichi in Chad, six hundred miles from the southern Algerian border. At the very least, it would be an opportunity to get intelligence data on the suspicious building and its true purpose.

At a remote Military base in Arizona, a team of technicians were instructed to prepare three quarters of a mile of small bore plastic hose, complete with three remotely initiated detonators. These were assembled on three sides of an old hangar building containing redundant test equipment. A party from Edwards Air force Base arrived with a super-cooled liquid in cryogenic containers marked "ASTROLITE G". The technicians were told that this fluid was an explosive with the fastest known detonation speed short of a nuclear explosion. The contents were discharged at ambient temperature into a receiver, and at exactly the right temperature, they were instructed to inject the fluid into the plastic tube until it flowed out from the far end. Wearing goggles and protective gloves, they sealed the tube with a simple bung, and withdrew to a command centre half a mile away. On initiation, there was a violent explosion followed by an extraordinary ripping sound, and when the smoke and dust cleared, only part of the fourth side of the building was visible. The old test rigs stored in the building had been totally destroyed by less than three gallons of this fluid. The floor area was covered in fused metal parts whose molecular structure was completely disrupted, looking for all the world like exotic coral. The observers were deeply shocked and impressed. A film record was made of the test. They were then shown a film of an earlier test where a tube about the size of a pencil, filled with this explosive and stuck upright in the sand, was detonated beneath an old army battle tank. The turret of the tank was blown twenty feet into the air.

"Our solution is at hand gentlemen", said the director of the test.

In the United Nations the Secretary General implored the nations to remain calm and to arrive at an acceptable solution, but the situation continued to be un-resolved and the secret Joint Security Committee decided to accelerate and escalate activities in Africa.

Sergeants Gil Lamont, Valery Stensis, and an SAS soldier named Bill received movement orders to report as civilians to Algiers, where they would be met by a contact in the Algerian Army who would brief them. A technical specialist from the United States would then supply them with explosives dedicated for a task to be revealed only when they were en route for the target.

At the remote military base in Arizona, an un-marked C17 was prepared for a flight to Djanet in southern Algeria, previously known as Fort Charlet and now used as a point of access to the Algerian National Park of Tassili-n-Ajja. This flight by Air America would require in-flight refuelling by KC135 Air Refuelling Tankers over the Cape Verde Islands. Two tankers were positioned at Ascension Island, some two thousand miles to the south. The C17 was to carry the cryogenic tanks containing the Astrolite G and its associated equipment to be used by the covert team within the group of military advisors to the African Task Force. Its purpose, and as far as practical its existence, was to be kept from all except the covert group within the advisors. This was possible because the use of small cryogenic containers known as Dewers enabled the safe transport of the frozen liquid, which when decanted at ambient conditions into the insulated three gallon receiver tank, expanded to give ample liquid explosive.

Chapter 11
OPERATION "DEEP CLEAN"

Armentrude was distressed . . . she had that awful feeling again . . . she could not decide if it was worry, a sense of guilt, or stupid self pity . . . or was it concern, or rather love for Gil?

That morning, her Section Chief had asked her to contact Gil at her apartment, and to tell him to report to an un-marked building a few metres down the street from Interpol Paris.

She knew what this meant.

In Castlewood House in London, Giles Greenaway was mildly excited. He had conceived a truly outrageous plan which flagrantly disregarded all diplomatic attempts to prevent the spread of high tech chemical and biological weapons. He intended to use a perfectly proper operation by African Nations to restore law and order in Southern Sahara, to mask a covert attempt to eliminate the terrorist efforts to develop this technology. If he, with support from America and France managed to succeed, there would be a cloak of diplomatic silence on the matter ; but if they failed, or even if they succeeded and were detected, the international repercussions would be immense. The

Hadleigh Frobisher Committee was completely in the dark about this development.

Giles began to think of an explanation for release should the destruction of the target be successful. How could the instant destruction of a whole building complex be explained when no known weapons had been deployed? He had one more outrageous trick up his sleeve, but he set that aside for now, and metaphorically held his breath, waiting for developments.

In the un-marked Paris building, Gil received his movement orders and airline ticket for Algiers. He was to travel light in civilian clothes with a single overnight bag. At the airport he would be met by someone from the Algerian Army, and he would then be under their control until contacted by specialists from the United States who would inform him of the true reason for his presence in the African Task Force. He was told that he would be in the company of some of his colleagues in a recent action. Their previous association, and the reason for them being assembled within the team of military advisors was to be kept secret from the rest of those present. More information would be provided in due course, and in the meantime, they should give the Africans every possible assistance in their mission.

Armentrude watched Gil leave the building from her office window. She felt sick with worry, and wanted to rush out and tell him not to go. She had no idea where he was going, or what his involvement entailed, but she just knew that he would be surrounded by potentially hostile people, and at risk until he returned.

What made people like him volunteer for work like this? she thought, and then realised that in fact, she had herself voluntarily and gladly accepted a career in this shady business because she had been unable to get any other work with satisfactory pay.

The same applies to Gil, she realised, but there was more to it than that, she knew that both she and he were proud to be involved in the frustration of those intent on true evil in the name of religion, or for any other reason.

The Task Force being assembled at Algiers, they embarked on a fleet of ten ancient Nord Nor-Atlas aircraft. The military advisors were unarmed and told that they were there to act as final approvers of operational plans by this multi-national group. Like referees, this would prevent undue rivalry between the soldiers of the four African nations involved.

Gil met Stensis and Bill, and all three quietly integrated with advisors in the Task Force, and awaited contact and briefing from the specialist from the United States.

The ageing piston-engined transports took off and headed for Djanet, some 1200 miles away in the south east corner of Algeria. Gil wondered about their range fully loaded, realising that there were no possible diversions after half way. However the faithful old aircraft completed the cold, unpressurised, noisy journey in seven hours, flying at twelve thousand feet over a desperately inhospitable terrain. At Djanet they assembled in a military camp and were formed into four patrols comprising three all-terrain vehicles carrying eight men, with an advisor in each vehicle.

The C17 arrived from Arizona late in the first evening, and Gil, Stensis and Bill managed to get on board without attracting attention.

Within the massive aircraft, they were shown videos of the target buildings near Kichi Kichi in Chad, and the films of the Astrolite G tests. They were instructed on how it was to be deployed round the target . . . that mysterious building complex. They got to handle the cryogenic containers, the receiver, stainless steel hand pump, stopper for the tube end and detonators using protective gloves and safety goggles. After several dry runs, they stowed the equipment in back packs, and left them in a cool chamber within the aircraft. They were given Glock hand guns and hand held GPS sets with the co-ordinates of the target already entered. These same instruments could send out a distress signal for IFF, location and emergency extraction. They each had special cell phones with open channel selection and satellite connection to a secret comms centre. Finally, they had a session in which they tried to predict possible problems arising *after* detonating the Astrolite G. A major consideration was to ensure that all of the components were destroyed in the explosion, especially the cryogenic containers and receiver. They should then get clear and attempt to rejoin their patrol during the likely confusion after detonation. Drones should be expected, so their GPS locator and IFF signals should be ON, to avoid attack. Stensis, who was still alive due to his innate caution, requested a spare GPS set in case of failure. Returning to their camp, they waited to see how the Task Force would deploy them, and if or when they might get near the target during patrols.

Giles Greenaway now decided to retreat to his villa at Deadman`s Cay in the Bahamas. Whist en-route in his Gulfstream 3000, he invited Admiral Walter Revere USN to join him, but the admiral was a cautious man and replied that he had other engagements. US Army General Sherman Blund was not so shy however, and arranged for some well deserved leave. Accordingly, in this most congenial location, they set up a monitoring and control centre with the ability to insert instructions to the drone operators in the Pentagon Ops. Center.

On the fifth day of patrols across Niger and into Chad, a Ganjaweed gang was detected heading towards an area with parched vegetation in which there was a group of huts, some goats and a few native families scraping an existence from this forbidding landscape. The Task Force Commander ordered a hot pursuit of the terrorists.

"I guess a cool chase is out of the question", said Gil, noting that at mid-day it was 51°C.

"A cool chase is not at all cool!", replied the African officer in the vehicle, failing to catch the intended humour.

He is a bit tense, thought Gil as they bounced over the rough terrain, with Bill and Stensis in the other two vehicles. Stensis carried the receiver and pump, and Bill had the plastic tube and detonator kit.

Gil was worried that the special dewers in his pack were getting warmer, and there was a distinct chemical smell emanating from it. He checked his GPS, and noted that they were some eight miles from the likely destination of the Ganjaweed gang, and that was about fifteen miles short of the target site.

Ahead, stretching across the track from north to south was an area of sand dunes beyond which was the settlement, which from the noise of gunfire was being attacked by the Ganjaweed. Gil was in the lead vehicle with the African patrol commander as they burst out of the dunes and into immediate contact with the terrorists who were ransacking the settlement, hell-bent on rape and pillage. They were so engrossed in this that most of them did not notice that they were being attacked at first, but those that did opened fire on the lead task force vehicle, disabling it. A firefight with hand-to-hand combat broke out between the Task Force and the Ganjaweed, who fled by truck and on foot.

The Task Force commander and his troops left their disabled vehicle and transferred to the two remaining to continue the chase, leaving Gil, Stensis and Bill to tend to the wounded. Gil was sickened by the senseless savagery. Besides the dead, there were many wounded, some screaming in burning huts. Slaughtered children and livestock lay about, but worse still was a dying mother who had been slashed by several machete blows to her head and chest, raped and mutilated. Her screaming baby crawling in the gore of her breasts. Flashes of Mary-Jane assailed him, but he forced himself to assist the wounded and extinguish the burning huts by shovelling sand onto the base of the fires.

Stensis and Bill changed the left front wheel and made an emergency repair to the radiator of the damaged patrol vehicle, which they refilled with water from the patrol's drinking water supplies. Meanwhile, Gil located the medical kit and gave first aid to the wounded until all the bandages, morphine and disinfectant were used up. Bill said they were as good to go as he could make it, so the three of them drove off towards their objective before the return of the rest of the Task Force.

After ten miles of driving off-piste, the engine began to overheat and lose power. Now they could see their objective, a large industrial building, surrounded by the debris of construction which would provide ample cover for preparation of their special explosive.

The vehicle struggled on for a few more miles and then the engine expired, so they disembarked, and taking all their kit, began to walk towards the target.

The sun was now setting, and it would get dark and quite cold very soon . . .

A blessed relief, thought Gil, so they each took bearings on the target and trudged on. There was none of the usual soldiers` crack, each was engrossed in the details of his part in the task ahead.

A sudden screaming rush of air, and they all fell flat on the ground which was mixed rocks, pebbles and sand . . .

"What the hell was that?", gasped Bill.

They strained their eyes to see something which might have caused their alarm . . .

"Look up guys", said Gil, and they saw the sun flash on the wings of a drone as it turned.

"Quickly, switch on your IFF", yelled Stensis, as the drone came in on a decelerating run.

They struggled to select the right function on their GPS sets, and they all succeeded.

The drone passed quietly over them, waggling its wings about a hundred feet above in recognition . . .

Gil rolled over onto his pack and said with great relief, "Thank heavens someone knows where we are!"

The drone climbed away in a wide spiral and was quickly lost to view.

The last mile and a half were completed in darkness, and they took cover in an area of piles of scrap building materials. They paused to drink high energy drinks and rations, before starting to prepare the equipment.

Gil`s pack was positively steaming, or rather almost smoking, and threatened to ignite, so they took out the dewers and hoped that the rapidly dropping night temperatures would ease the situation.

"We should decant them into the receiver as soon as possible before they blow us all to vapour!", said Bill.

They needed no encouragement, and the crisis was averted.

Now Stensis fitted the detonators into the plastic tube in four equi-distant positions which would locate one on each side of the main building. To do this, he had to run out the four lengths of tube in straight lines, locate the receptacles and insert the detonators. He left the safety caps on the detonators and Bill wound the lengths of tube diagonally round his shoulders, but there was too much for one person, so Stensis did the same with the rest.

"We are much too close", said Bill, and to Gil he said, "can you look for somewhere about half a mile back from here so we don`t get scorched".

"I can see a good spot over there beyond those trucks . . . that pile of gravel. Bill you and Stensis run the plastic tube round the building, and I will carry the empty dewers in their pack, and the full receiver to the end of the tube circuit beside the building like we rehearsed. I don`t have to remind you to remove the detonator safety caps as you go! While you pump the fluid into the tube, I will take the initiator set over to that pile of gravel and shine my torch so that you can see to come back quickly. Bill,

I take it that you will want the pleasure of pressing the button . . . Let`s do it!"

It took thirty three minutes to set-up the tube as close to the building footings as possible. There were no patrols or sentries, and no external activity, only a humming sound showed that the building was active. Bill and Stensis connected one end to the pump and receiver, and Gil started to pump while they got their breath back. He then left them pumping and headed for the mound of gravel. Bill and Stensis took turns at pumping, and after twenty minutes, Astrolite G oozed out of the open end of the tube. Stensis donned his gloves and goggles, and inserted the bung into the tube end. Placing the empty receiver beside the building, they headed for Gil`s light, shining from the pile of gravel.

Fifteen minutes later, the three of them lay behind the gravel pile, pulses racing.

Bill prepared the initiator set with its aerials positioned to give a wide arc signal towards the building when the firing button was pressed . . . Still no sign of sentries or patrols . . .

"Ready?", said Bill, "keep your head down and your eyes closed with your goggles and gloves on. Stay well below the rim of the mound, as the thermal shock will precede the pressure wave and then this shit will fly all over the place, and we are not very well protected, so best of luck . . . what do you yanks say? . . . *Fire in the hole!*", and he pressed the button.

There was an almighty flash and a blast of heat, followed by a whining, ripping sound and an ear-splitting triple bang like thunder. Gravel stung their bodies, and they were thrown backwards some thirty feet.

Gil kept his eyes tight shut, his ears were singing, and his head spinning . . . after several long seconds he opened his eyes and looked up. A great column of black smoke showed against the stars in the night sky, and particles of something, some of which were sort of sticky began to fall on everything . . . The gravel pile had mostly gone, as had the building. Now there was only a smouldering area of fused metal with sputtering fires.

"Let's Get The hell out of here!" . . . It was Stensis' voice, "are you all right guys?"

"Let's go", said Bill.

"Roger that", said Gil, and they ran towards the farthest truck from the blast area.

To everyone's amazement it started with a bit of encouragement from Bill with the wires to the ignition switch. The only problem was that there was no viable track from the lorry park to the direction from which they had come, so they drove away south as fast as they could.

Back in the Bahamas, Giles Greenaway and General Sherman Blund watched with awe and admiration rather than shock.

"Let's have a cup of tea", said Giles, as he switched from the drone to the satellite which was just coming on-line as it passed over the Southern Sahara.

"The drone will mop-up all survivors".

"What about our guys?", said Blund.

"Oh I'm sure that they will be OK, I'll arrange an extraction for them later if they need it".

In Paris, Armentrude was numb with anxiety. She had never experienced that level of concern and terror before. She could not sleep and she was sick when even thinking of food. After a while she realised that she was also sick every morning . . .

Oh no! she thought, *what if?* . . .

In the United Nations they were still arguing about whether the buildings were in fact a medicine factory or were something more sinister, when the Russian delegate announced that the building complex had apparently been destroyed. After the uproar had subsided, the Secretary General asked if any delegates could suggest how this might have occurred.

No further information being forthcoming, Her Majesty`s delegate announced on behalf of NATO, that no missiles, cruise or otherwise, and no bombing missions had been fired or flown by NATO Forces. The delegate for South Africa then declared on behalf of the Organisation of African Nations, that no attacks had been made on the facility by African forces, whatever it may have been used for.

Heading south in Chad in the commandeered lorry, Gil asked Stensis who was driving,

"Why are we still going south?"

Stensis replied, "I am skirting round the sand dunes to the west of us, and then I propose to head north to intercept the Task Force patrol`s tracks, and head back to the base at Djanet. We have plenty of fuel, and it will be dawn in about half an hour. We are on a fairly hard surface here, but in the dunes we would leave tracks, and it is harder to keep on course. We need if possible to seem to be coming from an entirely different direction from that of our target".

This seemed sensible to Gil and Bill, and all three were silent until Bill noticed that the sand and dust on his clothing was slightly sticky, and he began to experience an increasing itchiness. When he tried to dust it off, it balled-up and as it got lighter as the day dawned, he saw that it was scorching his clothing. He looked at Gil and Stensis and let out a horrified yell . . .

"What the hell is this shit? . . . Look at your faces!"

"Jesus, you don't look too good yourself" said Gil, and as the sun warmed them, all three began to itch and feel nauseous. Stensis said that he could not see clearly and began to slow down, but too late, he drove over a large rock piercing the sump of the engine which quickly seized and the truck stopped.

Now they were all in extreme pain. Their lips cracked and turned black, they could hardly see, and blisters formed between their fingers and toes. Their eyes stung and their nose and sinuses were blocked or discharging. They were nauseous and had difficulty breathing.

"Bill, find the EPIRB switch on your GPS and switch it on. I will continue to transmit the IFF signal on mine. Stensis, switch yours off to save juice. That will give us maximum battery life and signals", said Gil. "We have enough water for about another day and some".

They could hear a drone, but were unable to see it or anything much.

"If you get out to piss, don't wander off. Keep in the shade", said Stensis.

Bill added, "conserve energy and just concentrate on keeping your vital functions going"

"I don't have many left", said Stensis.

"What are those when they are at home?", croaked Gil.

"Seriously guys, humour is good, but it takes energy, so just rest, and hopefully we will be extracted".

In Giles Greenaway`s villa in the Bahamas, Giles and General Blund finished a leisurely dinner and strolled into the room in which the satellite comms had been installed, and watched the drones take out all moving targets within a five mile radius of the target.

Secretly, Giles was aware that the African Task Force soldiers did not have IFF.

"Where are our guys then?", asked General Blund.

"Oh they are well clear by now", replied Giles.

"No need for a special extraction then?", asked Blund . . .

"No,I don`t think so, they are probably back in base, but I will check in the morning", said Giles, who had no such intention.

Chapter 12
RESCUE, RECOVERY, AND RETALIATION?

In the control room of a military base in Israel, the MATZ officer noticed an EPIRB signal from the Sub-Saharan region, but this one was not from any registered source. Nevertheless, as he knew that Mossad and Israeli special forces were operating in the Central African Republic and Chad, he notified them, partly because he was bored.

In Nokou, north of Lake Chad, Israeli Air Force Lieutenant Yuri Thorniloe was airborne with sufficient fuel in his Yanshuf helicopter. His controller notified him of the EPIRB signal and he tuned in his receiver. Flying at 200 knots, he was overhead in 55 minutes. He saw a stationary truck with a trail of black oil behind it. Landing his chopper close by, his crew members reported three casualties in the truck. They were alive, but clearly distressed and incoherent. Lieutenant Thorniloe reported that the casualties might be contagious, and stood-by for instructions. He was told to recover the three men, but those assisting them were to minimise contact, use gloves and wear their combat smoke masks.

Gil, Stensis and Bill were by then unconscious, and unaware that they were being rescued. They were flown to a secret destination and transferred into an Israeli C130 transport in which they were given life support whilst being flown to Israel. Arriving at Tel-Aviv, they were quickly transferred to the Sagol School of Neuroscience, under the supervision of Professor Henri Zinn whose task was to determine what reagents had caused their symptoms, and to perform if possible, the necessary recovery treatment. It was quickly apparent that a number of vital functions were failing, and rapid organ replacement was necessary to sustain life. Doctor Ilia Zagreb of the TAU Center for Nanoscience was consulted, but the patients` identity and medical history could not be identified, and although eminently suitable for treatment, no viable means of funding this expensive work existed. The patients remained on life support for several days while their identity was sought.

The sudden appearance of a senior Mossad Officer resolved the funding issue, and the Nano-neurosurgeons were told that these men were agents of national importance and that their recovery was vital in the fight against terrorism. They had no idea how true that really was . . . After detoxification, the lengthy process began, all three responding better than expected to the experimental treatment which replaced their retinas, clarified the fluid within the eyes, and repaired the lens and iris with steroid injections. Nano Contacts at the nerve junctions within their central nervous system improved synapse performance, speeding up their reactions. Nano regulators were placed in their heart and respiratory centres. Glandular operations on the thyroid and pituitary glands were intended to improve their endurance, but only time would tell if that was successful.

On regaining consciousness, they experienced confusion and loss of balance initially, but after three days they all declared that they needed exercise, so they were sent to the gymnasium for stamina and reaction tests. The results were outstanding, but the improvement if any, was not quantifiable because their original fitness was not known.

Bill reminded them that they had been involved in a covert mission, and that their identity was best kept secret, even from Mossad, so they all pretended to have loss of memory.

In Paris, Armentrude was beside herself with worry.

Mon Dieu, aidez-eux, she prayed every waking second.

She had very little sleep, and her Section Chief told her to go home, but she was adamant that she must stay to get any possible news as soon as it was received.

Her nausea continued, especially in the morning, and she knew that she was pregnant.

She sought the assistance of Giles Greenaway who replied,

"As far as I know, Sergeant Gil Lamont is still on operations for the United Nations with the Organisation of African Nations' Task Force in the Southern Sahara area, and it is not possible to locate or communicate with him. You must contact the United Nations".

An Interpol colleague who was possibly Jewish whispered, "You might do better to ask Commandant Pintonen of the Foreign Legion, or failing that, try my friend in Israel who I suspect is a Mossad Agent".

Armentrude contacted Commandant Pintonen, and was even more disturbed when he said that he also was concerned, as he had had no report from Senior Sergeant Valery Stensis. He thought that contacting Mossad was a good idea, and he promised to do so immediately.

Within the hour, Mossad confirmed that they had recovered three Caucasian male persons from an area north of Lake Chad, who had been found unconscious but alive.

These men were now in hospital in Tel-Aviv, and were recovering well, but their identities were unknown.

Without hesitation and without permission, Armentrude took the next flight from Charles de Gaulle to Tel-Aviv, where she met her Mossad contact at the airport.

With the assistance of Commandant Pintonen, they were flown back to Calvi within two days. No record of their transfer was made either in Israel or Corsica.

In the United Nations General Assembly, the death of an entire patrol of the African Task Force was attributed to a Ganjaweed Terrorist Group. Questions were raised concerning the destruction of a new medicine factory in Chad. Accusations were pointed at the United States, Great Britain, and even Russia, but all denied firing any missiles or bombing the area.

In a press release, discretely leaked by "official sources", it was claimed that certain parts of the Southern Sahara were prone to meteorite strikes, and the popular press asked,

"Are we being attacked by aliens?"

This heralded the gradual loss of interest in the subject by the thinking public who were more interested in the forthcoming Olympics.

The Hadleigh Frobisher Committee congratulated Giles Greenaway for his part in resolving their concerns so satisfactorily, but he modestly denied any part in it. He expressed deep regret concerning the fate of three of the Military Advisors who were now presumed dead. Nevertheless, he appeared in the New Years Honours List.

As for the three survivors, Bill returned to his wife and children in Herefordshire, Senior Sergeant Stensis was promoted to Warrant Officer and addressed as Mon Adjudant Stensis, and Gil Lamont was happily re-united with Armentrude in the family apartment in Calvi, where he learned that he was to become a father!

Armentrude was delighted to have Gil back safe and apparently well, and she was even more pleased when he declared with great conviction . . .

"Never again! Never Again! . . . Never volunteer" . . .

However, he was somehow different she thought . . . very fit and almost hyperactive.

He never could settle down before, but now he was clearly restless. Something was bugging him!

Gil said that he must stay fit, and each day he timed himself as he ran round the beach of Calvi Bay to the far end, and swam back across the Bay to where he started from. He seemed obsessive about improving his time.

"What are you training for?", she asked . . . "You said no more soldiering".

"I got to set things right", he said.

"What things?"

"You don't need to know", he said.

"You will soon be a father, and I will need you around so that I can go to work", said Armentrude. "You can write your book and look after our baby!" . . .

Gil shuddered, he had not planned for this, and he certainly did not feel like settling down.

"I will not be a soldier, but I have a score to settle".

"Why?" she asked.

"Someone tried to kill us, or at least put us in harm's way in the desert. I know who it was and I am going to punish him severely".

"Don't do anything stupid, you have to think like a parent, if not a husband".

"Is that what is bugging you? Is marriage that important these days?"

"Of course it is", she said.

"Well I am going away for about two weeks soon, and when I return, we can think about getting married".

"If that is a proposal, it's not very romantic!"

"Who said I was romantic? . . . No it was not a proposal, I guess I will do that when I come back, and if all goes well, I will feel much more relaxed, and well . . . more romantic!".

Armentrude was not very reassured by that, and Gil realised that he would have to make it up to her somehow. He wondered if all veteran soldiers felt as disturbed as he did.

He could not imagine a settled domestic existence after the trauma of the last month or so, but he could not help himself. It was as if he might self-destruct! . . . A stupid argument.

Now, as a double veteran, Gil found he could not settle down. He could not get his mind round the news that he was going to be a father. There was no sign of pregnancy yet, and he did not have the sort of job that requires a daily routine to keep his mind in line. He was angry, very angry. His nature was such that he would not resort to criminal violence against persons, but his frustrations might well be directed at their property.

The experience of experimental surgery in Tel-Aviv without which he would certainly have died, had been performed when he was unconscious and close to death. He knew nothing of the procedures, or their likely effect on his physique or his mind. Their side effects were to a degree responsible for his current demeanour.

In the morning, he told Armentrude that he loved her, and that she was not to worry but he would be away for just less than two weeks. He flew to Paris and on to Nassau the next day. At Nassau he chartered a fishing boat with skipper, after making a search for the right kind of outfit . . . the sort of skipper and boat which could be persuaded to entertain dubious activities for a good cash settlement, and keep his mouth shut.

They sailed the same day, and motored the two hundred miles to Deadman`s Cay over the next four days. Dexter Main, the skipper did not ask questions, he just took his boat wherever Gil wanted.

Giles Greenaway was in London, enjoying the pleasure of entertainment by Lord Skidestie and the other members of the Hadleigh Frobisher Committee, who had been celebrating their success lavishly, but without publicity at the country estate of another member.

Just before sundown off Giles`villa on Deadman`s Cay, Gil slipped quietly into the sea and swam ashore. He had been observing all day to check that nobody was in residence. Approaching the main building, he found a hoe and some outboard gasoline in a shed full of garden tools and boating equipment, and forced an entrance through a patio door. Inside, he splashed gasoline over a couple of bedrooms, and in the open living area, he turned on and lit the grill, and just before leaving, opened the valve on a spare bottle of propane gas. He had time to swim back to the boat before observing the satisfying fireball as the premises were destroyed.

On the return journey they were stopped by a maritime police patrol about twenty miles short of Nassau, but said that they were only on a local fishing trip. Boarding the boat, the policemen found nothing unusual, and let them continue without checking their ID. Gil had told the skipper that his name was John Savoury.

On landing at Nassau, Gil paid-off the skipper and took the next local flight to South Caicos in the Turks and Caicos Islands, and from there flew on a chartered light aircraft to the Dominican Republic. From Santo Domingo, he took a Russian Airline flight to Brussels, and returned by train to Paris and Armentrude who was very pleased to see him, and found that he was much more relaxed . . . more like he was when they first met.

The man in the grey suit and spectacles reported that Gil had been in a private health centre on the outskirts of Brussels for the last two weeks since he had returned from Calvi.